The Littlest Snowman

E. J. Sullivan

Illustrated by

Judith Mitchell

SWEET WATER PRESS

The Littlest Snowman
Copyright © 2005 by Sweetwater Press
Produced by Cliff Road Books

ISBN 1-58173-382-8

Printed in Italy

The Littlest Snowman

Once upon a time in the South, a little girl and boy looked out their window and saw snowflakes falling.

The girl, Lily, and her brother, Bo, were excited. "Now that we have snow, Santa Claus will be sure to come!" Lily said. They ran outside to play.

There was just enough snow for the children to make a tiny snowman. All that night, the little snowman stood in Bo and Lily's yard. He looked up and down the street, wondering why there were no other snowmen. By morning, he knew. The snow was already melting!

Bo and Lily ran outside after breakfast and saw how warm it was. "Our snowman will melt!" Lily cried. Bo had an idea. They picked up the little snowman, ran into the house, and put him in the refrigerator.

The snowman heard Bo and Lily talking in the kitchen. Lily was crying. "The snow is all melting," she cried. "How will Santa ever come when there's no snow for his sleigh?"

The snowman had to do something to help. That night, he sneaked out of the house and went in search of more snow.

He hitched a ride on an ice cream truck. "Can you help me?" he asked the ice cream cones. But they shook their heads. "Santa can't land on ice cream," they said.

The snowman got on a train, in a railroad car full of ice cubes. "Can you help me?" he asked the ice cubes. "You need snow, not ice," they said.

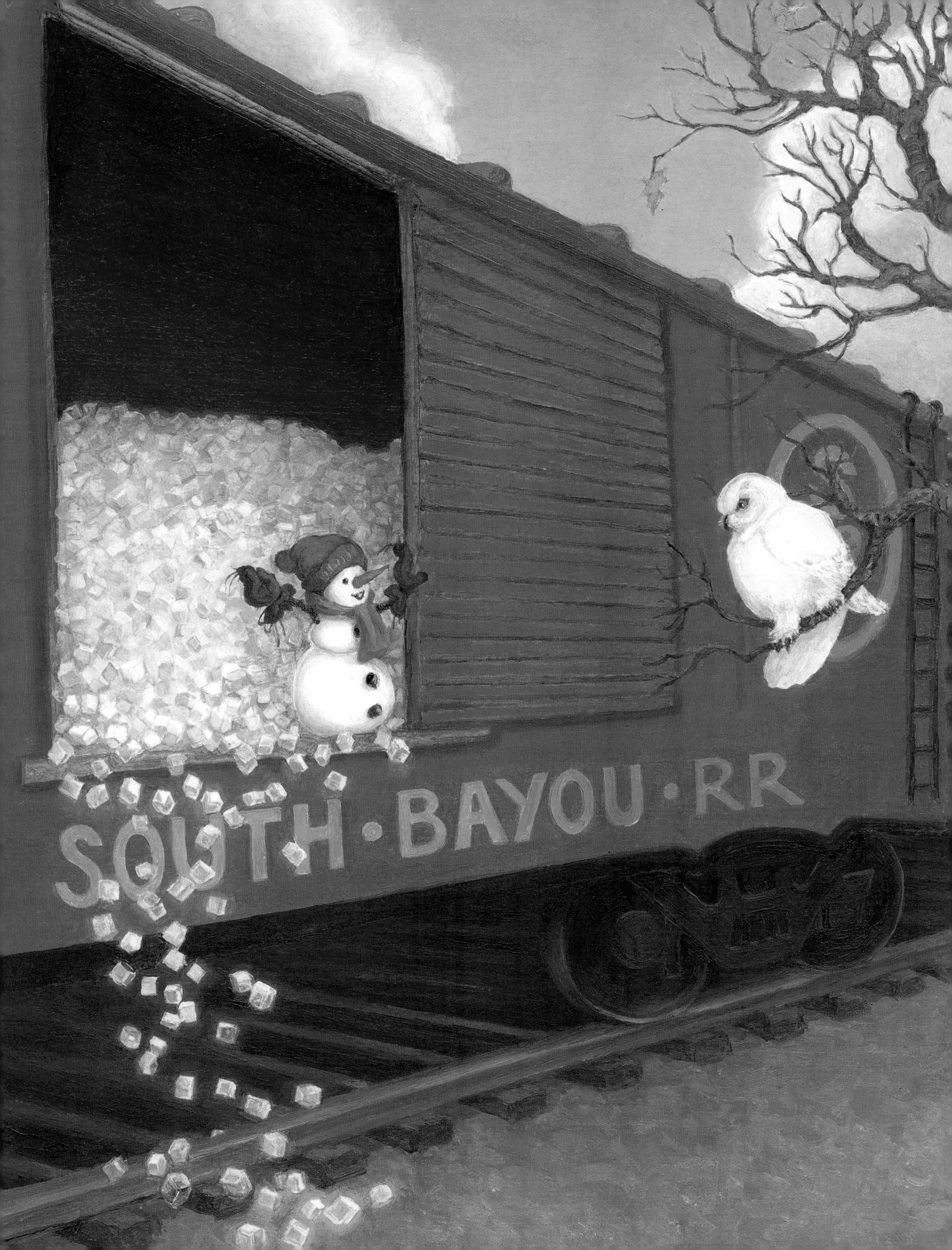
SOUTH • BAYOU • RR

"I have to get to the North Pole," the snowman decided. "That's where all the snow is."

When the train stopped, the snowman saw a big white bird. "You look like a snowbird," he said. "Can you fly me to the North Pole?"

"Hop on," the bird said. The little snowman scrambled onto the bird's back and away they flew.

At the North Pole, there were mountains of snow everywhere. Living in the mountains were snowmen of all sizes. Some were giants! The littlest snowman was afraid, but he thought about Bo and Lily and got up his courage. "Will you come to Bo and Lily's house?" he asked a giant snowman.

"No!" the snowman thundered. "GO HOME!"

The sad little snowman looked all over for
a friendly face, but no one would help.

Finally, he jumped on an iceberg, where a polar bear told him, "You better hurry. It's almost Christmas!"

The polar bear took the littlest snowman
to Christmastown, where Santa Claus lived.
The snowman hurried up to the house
and knocked on the door.
Mrs. Claus answered.
"You're too late," she said.
"It's Christmas Eve. Santa
has already left to visit all
the children."

The littlest snowman hung his head. He turned and slowly walked away. He was so sad he started to cry … and cry … and cry. The littlest snowman couldn't stop crying! His tears poured out. And as they flowed, they froze. They were turning into snowflakes! Piles and piles of snowflakes!

Suddenly there was a roar and a blast of cold air. It was the North Wind, on his way home. "Little snowman!" roared the North Wind. "Why are you crying?"

Between sobs, the littlest snowman told the North Wind his story. "I think I can help you," the North Wind said. "Just watch this. And hang on to your hat!"

The North Wind puffed out his big cheeks and blew.
He blew the littlest snowman up into the sky, along with
all his snowflake tears. The North Wind blew so hard,
he blew the littlest snowman, along with enough snow
to cover the whole South, all the way home.

Just as he was about to land at Bo and Lily's house, Santa Claus passed the snowman in his sleigh. "Oh, no!" cried the littlest snowman. "I'm too late!"

Santa Claus laughed. "Silly snowman," he said. "I don't need snow to land! Don't you know that when you have Christmas in your heart, Santa will always come?"

"But that snow you brought to the children will be the best gift of all," Santa said. "And because you are such a brave and true friend, I'm going to reward you."

Santa asked the North Wind to blow a big bubble around the littlest snowman and his snowflakes. The next thing the snowman knew, he was back in Bo and Lily's house in a place of honor on the mantel above the fireplace.

And there the littlest snowman would live forever in his beautiful crystal globe, with snow always falling around him, and Christmas always in his heart.